W9-AQO-899
DEC 1981
RECEIVED
OHIO DOMINICAN
COLLEGE LIBRARY
COLUMBUS, OHIO
43219

BING, BONG, BANG AND FIDDLE, DEE, DEE

Bing Bong Bang and Fiddle Dee Dee

BY GERDA MARTINBAND

Illustrated by Anne Rockwell

Doubleday & Company, Inc., Garden City, New York

Library of Congress Catalog Number 78-18562

ISBN 0-385-14211-0 Trade

ISBN 0-385-14212-9 Prebound

Printed in the United States of America

First Edition

For Julie and Katie Heffer

One day an old man

went to market

and brought a fiddle home.

"What's that for?"

asked his wife.

"It's for me to play

on Saturday nights,"

said the old man.

"It will put a bit of life into us."

"You can't play the fiddle,"

said the old woman.

"There's nothing to it,"

said the old man.

"I will learn fast."

On Saturday, animal music

was coming in the kitchen window.

"Neigh-neigh,

moo-moo,

baa-baa,

oink-oink,

cluck-cluck,

and cock-a-doodle-doo."

The old man took his fiddle.

"Scrape-scrape,"

he went

and "Squeak-squawk"

and "Fiddle, dee, dee."

"Ouch," said the old woman,

holding her ears.

The old man did not notice.

He fiddled on.

“I’ll give him some music,”

thought the old woman.

She went to the cupboard.

She took out a great stewpot.

And she took two wooden spoons

that were hanging on the wall.

“Bing, bong, bang,”

went the old woman

on the stewpot.

“Scrape, squeak,

and fiddle, dee, dee,”

went the old man on the fiddle.

The cat was angry.

She got up from the fireside.

“Meow, meow, meow,”

she said, and she left.

"Bing, bong, bang,"

and "Fiddle, dee, dee,"

went the old man and his wife.

"Grrr," said the dog

and followed the cat outside.

"Bing, bong, bang,"

and "Bingle-bongle,"

and "Scrape, squeak,"

and "Fiddle, deedle, deedle, dee,"

went the old man and his wife.

Each one tried to play

louder than the other.

Now animal voices

came in the window.

They sounded angry.

"What's up?" asked the old man.

He went to the window to look.

“Wife!” he cried.

“There goes Dobbin

over the barnyard wall!”

"Clip-clop,"

went the horse's hooves

as he ran away.

"What!" shouted the old woman.

She pushed the old man

from the window

and looked for herself.

"And there goes Bossy, husband,"

she cried.

"Thud."

The cow jumped after the horse.

The old man

burst through the kitchen door.

He saw the sheep take a flying leap

after the cow.

The rooster and the hen

ran after the sheep.

And the pig

waddled through the gate.

"Come back, come back,"

hollered the old man.

He ran after the animals.

“Wait for me, wait for me,”

yelled the old woman.

She trotted after the old man.

The old man shouted

over his shoulder,

"Now you've done it, wife,

with your bing, bong, banging.

If we don't catch the animals,

we won't have

any milk, butter, or eggs."

"And no wool or bacon,"

the old woman shouted.

"But it's your fault, not mine.

It's your fiddling that did it."

The animals ran down the road.

The old man and the old woman

ran after them.

Then big fat drops of rain

began to fall.

The rain fell faster and faster.

The animals huddled together

under a tree.

The old woman went after them.

"Come under the tree

with me, husband,"

she shouted.

A flash of lightning lit up the sky.

"Don't be a fool,"

the old man shouted back.

"A tree can be struck by lightning.

You come out of there."

But just then,

BANG!

A clap of thunder shook the tree.

The old woman threw her skirts

over her head

and didn't move.

The old man threw himself

on the ground.

He hid his head under his fiddle.

The horse rolled his eyes

and ran into the woods.

The cow, the pig, and the sheep jumped

through the bushes.

And the rooster and the hen

ran away.

Finally the thunder stopped.

"Plink, plonk."

The last two raindrops fell

on the old woman's nose.

The storm was over

and night had come.

The old woman looked

into the woods.

"See what you have done

with your scraping and squeaking

and your fiddle, dee, dee?"

she said.

"It wasn't me,"

said the old man.

"It was you with your

bing, bong, banging.

The animals liked *my* music."

The old man and the old woman stood there.

They were tired and wet.

Then the last clouds sailed away.

Silver moonlight

made the wet woods sparkle.

"We must find the animals,"

said the old man.

"You go this way,

and I'll go that way."

Among the trees it was dark again.

The old woman could hardly see

where she was going.

“Where are you, Dobbin?

Where are you, Bossy?”

she called.

But the cow and the horse

did not answer.

“It’s scary here at night,”

she thought.

“There are ghosts and goblins.

And witches, maybe.

I’d better go home.”

She turned around

and pushed some branches aside.

Her hand touched something

that was not a tree.

She stood still

and held her breath.

Woosh!

Some leaves moved.

Was it a robber?

Ssst!

Something ran across her feet.

She shook with fright.

Then a great sneeze made her jump.

"I know that sneeze,"

she said.

"Is it you, husband?"

"Is it you, wife?"

the old man answered.

They fell into each other's arms.

"Oh, husband!"

"Oh, wife!"

"Oh, wife!"

"Oh, husband!"

they said over and over.

"I bumped into something,"

said the old man.

"Into me," said the old woman.

"I thought you were a robber."

"I thought you were a goblin,"

said the old man.

"Let's go home,"

said the old woman.

"We can look for the animals

in the morning."

"You are right,"

said the old man.

"The morning is wiser

than the evening.

And the light is better too."

Hand in hand,

they went home.

And when they got there,

what did they see?

There was Dobbin trotting

into the barn.

And there was Bossy,

clomping after him.

The sheep was following them.

The rooster and the hen

were sitting in the barn.

The pig was eating his supper.

In the kitchen,

the dog and the cat

lay fast asleep.

“They have found

their own way home,”

cried the old man.

He lifted his fiddle to his chin.

"Now I'll play

a good-night song for them."

Oh, no you don't,"

cried the old woman.

"It would be good-bye

to the animals for sure.

We'll have no more

bing, bong, bang around here.

And no more scrape, squeak

and fiddle, dee, dee."

She took the old man's hand

and led him upstairs.

They got into bed

and went to sleep.

The next morning the old woman said,

"Did you hear the crickets last night?

They made so much noise!"

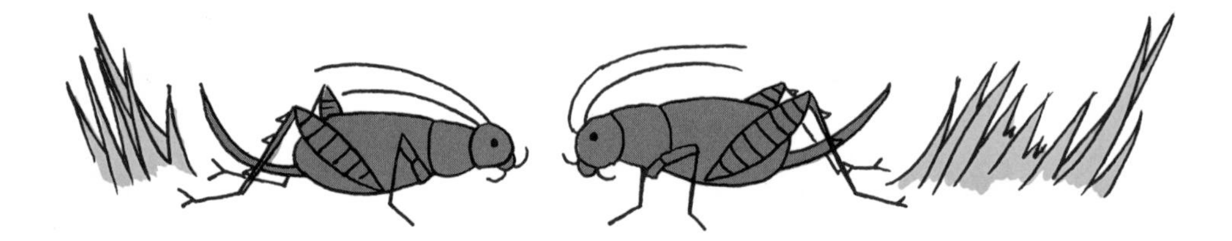

"No," said the old man,

"I didn't hear any crickets."

And two mornings later,

the old woman said,

"Didn't you hear the little mice

squeaking last night?"

"No," said the old man.

"I didn't hear any little mice."

And the morning after that,

she said,

"Did you hear the tree-toads

last night, husband?

They sang and sang."

"Is that right?"

said the old man.

"I didn't hear them."

On Saturday night,

the old man got out his fiddle.

"Oh, no,"

cried the old woman.

"The animals will run away again!"

But the old man began to play.

And he played

such a sweet tune

that the old woman

started dancing around the room.

And the animals came

and looked

in the window.

"When did you learn to play

so well, husband?"

asked the old woman.

"I practiced every night,"

said the old man.

"But you were in bed with me,"

said the old woman.

"No, I wasn't,"

said the old man.

"Then . . ."

said the old woman.

"That's right,"

said the old man.

"The crickets,

the little mice

and the tree toads—

they were all my fiddle!"

"Good," said the old woman.

"You can play all you like.

I don't mind,

and I don't think

the animals will either."

GERDA MARTINBAND taught kindergarten for many years at the Walden School and the Early Childhood Center at Brooklyn College. She lives in Brooklyn with her husband, and now devotes herself to writing and traveling. BING, BONG, BANG AND FIDDLE, DEE, DEE is her first book for Doubleday.

ANNE ROCKWELL'S beautiful illustrations have appeared in scores of children's books, many of which she has written herself. Among her recent books are *Gogo's Car Breaks Down* and *Gogo's Pay Day*. Anne lives with her family in Greenwich, Connecticut.

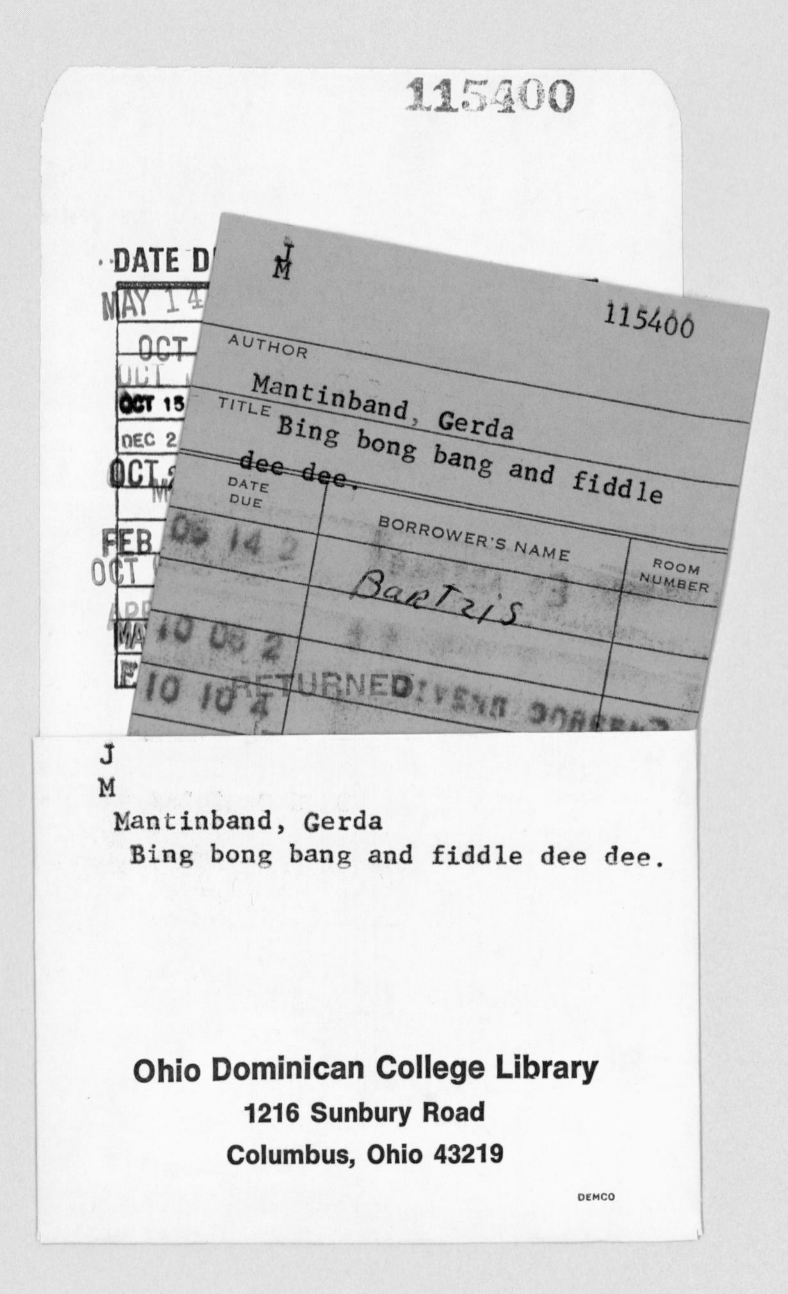

115400
DATE D
J
M
115400
AUTHOR
Mantinband, Gerda
TITLE
Bing bong bang and fiddle dee dee.
DATE DUE
BORROWER'S NAME
ROOM NUMBER
Bartzis
RETURNED